7.45

Untamed
Tongues

Wild Words
from
Wild Women

Autumn Stephens

Press
ey, CA

Printed in the United States of
America on recycled paper

Cover: Sharon Smith Design
Handlettering: Lilly Lee
Photograph courtesy of Receivership
of Mae West.

ISBN: 0-943233-51-8

Can We Talk?

Once we loved Barbie, the dishy doll with the missile-shaped bosoms and the pouty, slighty-parted plastic lips. Unfortunately, little Miss Implant didn't have much to say for herself: she was too busy trying on all those cunning size 1/2 costumes (though I think she did occasionally emit a coy giggle when Ken tried to get cuddly).

Then came Chatty Cathy, flagrantly flat-chested and corporeally quite charmless—but oh, how that baby could babble! We pulled her string and pulled her string, until one sad day her motor-mouth simply sputtered and died, never again to blurt out those startling, solipsistic demands for juice or a journey to the zoo.

Finally, we fell for Madonna, a self-proclaimed boy-toy

(though obviously she liked girls just fine too) who proved that you could have mammary glands *and* a jaw that opens all the way. "Listen," she said, "everyone is entitled to my opinion." And just in case we didn't think her smile was smug enough already, she wrapped it around a coke bottle to prove her point.

This book is for Andrea's daughter, and Margaret's, and all the other little Madonna-ettes who will, I hope, grow up knowing how to do more with their breasts than beat them, and more with their mouths than paint them stop-sign red.

Untamed Tongues

Garrulous
Goddesses

I'm tough, ambitious, and I know exactly what I want. If that makes me a bitch, okay.

—**Madonna**, *chameleon-esque queen of chutzpah.*

Success didn't spoil me; I've always been insufferable.

—*Satirist* **Fran Lebowitz**, *an inspiration to every sarcastic smart-ass who ever got herself booted out of high school.*

The Jews have produced only three originative geniuses: Christ, Spinoza, and myself.

It takes a lot of time to be a genius, you have to sit around so much doing nothing, really doing nothing.

Besides Shakespeare and me, who do you think there is?

—Writer **Gertrude Stein,** *who loomed large in the avant-garde circles of her day, and larger still in the privacy of her own mind.*

4

Just being in a room with myself is almost more stimulation than I can bear.

–**Kate Braverman**, *agitated author of the cult classic* Lithium for Medea.

I would live in a communist country providing I was the Queen.

–**Stella Adler**, *Methodic mentor to big screen kings Marlon Brando, Warren Beatty and Robert De Niro. ("If she were a character in a Greek play," one interviewer concluded, "her flaw would be hubris.")*

I have a horror of death; the dead are so soon forgotten. But when I die, they'll have to remember me.

—**Emily Dickinson**, *a poet far too singular to slip anybody's mind.*

The more articulate one is, the more dangerous words become.

—*Prolific poet/prosaist* **May Sarton**, *a major menace to society.*

If you haven't got anything nice to say about anybody, come sit next to me.

—**Alice Roosevelt Longworth**, *one of America's nastiest national institutions.*

Show me someone who never gossips, and I'll show you someone who isn't interested in people.

—*Broadcast newswoman* **Barbara Walters**, *a very caring conversationalist.*

Learning to speak is like learning to shoot.

—*Professor* **Avital Ronell**, *comparative literature specialist, and a self-proclaimed "ivory-tower terrorist."*

The people I'm furious with are the women's liberationists. They keep getting up on soap boxes and proclaiming that women are brighter than men. It's true but it should be kept quiet or it ruins the whole racket.

—*Screenwriter* **Anita Loos**, *who maintained that gentlemen were incapable of appreciating either brunettes or the basic facts of life.*

I wasn't allowed to speak while my husband was alive, and since he's gone no one has been able to shut me up.

Nobody's interested in sweetness and light.

—God-like gossip columnist **Hedda Hopper**. *With a flick of her poisonous pen, she could write a Hollywood hopeful right out of the picture.*

I think if women would indulge more freely in vituperation, they would enjoy ten times the health they do. It seems to me they are suffering from repression.

So long as women are slaves, men will be knaves.

–Elizabeth Cady Stanton,
the strapping spokeswoman for nineteenth-century suffragists.

Be critical. Women have the right to say: This is surface, this falsifies reality, this degrades.

—**Tillie Olsen**. *After twenty years of transcribing other people's words, the long-suppressed author of* Silences *finally found her own voice.*

My goal is to be accused of being strident.

—**Susan Faludi**, *scribe of the stinging* Backlash.

11

Raving

Beauties

I don't have the time every day to put on makeup. I need that time to clean my rifle.

–Henriette Mantel, *cosmetically incorrect comedian.*

My fame has enabled me to torture more formidable men.

–Actress **Sharon Stone**, *publicly pilloried as a "heartless" homewrecker. (Is* Basic Instinct *to blame?)*

You'd be surprised how much it costs to look this cheap.

It's a good thing that I was born a woman, or I'd have been a drag queen.

–Dolly Parton, *rags-to-riches country music mogul. (In her dimestore days, desperate Dolly saved face by rouging her lips with Mercurochrome.)*

I'm tired of all this non-sense about beauty being only skin-deep. That's deep enough. What do you want, an adorable pancreas?

—**Jean Kerr**, *perfectly attractive playwright whose modest goal was "to make a lot of people laugh and to make a lot of money."*

Taking joy in life is a woman's best cosmetic.

—**Rosalind Russell**, *minimalist "Auntie Mame" who also suffered from the misconception that an appealing lunch could be fashioned solely from an assortment of cheeses.*

Nature has made women with a bosom, so nature thought it was important. Who am I to argue with nature?

–Ida Rosenthal, *inventor of the modern brassiere. She figured out how to gently lift and separate the women from the girls.*

My husband said he wanted to have a relationship with a redhead, so I dyed my hair red.

–Activist/film star **Jane Fonda***, capable of changing her colors at the drop of an aerobics sock.*

I've never been lifted. But I do like a bit of glamour in the morning.

—Artist **Louise Nevelson**. *She preferred to be the sculptor, not the sculpture.*

Any girl can be glamorous. All you have to do is stand still and look stupid.

—**Hedy Lamarr**. *A much-coveted property pursuant to her elegantly unclad performance in the 1933 film Ecstasy, lovely Lamarr was smarter than she looked.*

I have too many fantasies to be a housewife . . . I guess I *am* a fantasy.

I've been on a calendar, but never on time.

I have never quite understood this sex symbol business, but if I'm going to be a symbol of something, I'd rather have it sex than some of the other things they've got symbols for.

—Marilyn Monroe, *dead movie star. Was too much feminine mystique her fatal mistake?*

It is possible that blondes also prefer gentlemen.

—**Mamie Van Doren,** *the other platinum bombshell of the fifties.*

I dress for women, and undress for men.

—**Angie Dickinson** *In or out of uniform, TV's leggy "Police Woman" inspired illicit fantasies.*

Think of me as a sex symbol for the men who don't give a damn.

—Comedian **Phyllis Diller**. *At the age of seventy-three, Ms. Diller posed as a poster girl for San Francisco's public transportation system, thereby also becoming a symbol for commuters who didn't give a damn if they showed up for work on time.*

A comparison between Madonna and me is a comparison between a strapless evening gown and a gownless evening strap.

–**Kim Campbell**, *Prime Minister of Canada, criticized for emulating America's sexy boy-toy when she bared her forty-six-year-old shoulders in a pre-election photo.*

Women should try to increase their size rather than decrease it, because I believe the bigger we are, the more space we'll take up, and the more we'll have to be reckoned with. I think every woman should be fat like me.

—Roseanne Arnold, *outsized sit-com star known both for her cheeky charm and for the cheeks themselves, revealed to an entire stadium of World Series fans during a 1989 mooning spree.*

A diet counselor once told me that all overweight people are angry with their mothers and channel their frustrations into overeating. So I guess that means all thin people are happy, calm, and have resolved their Oedipal entanglements.

—Wendy Wasserstein, *perpetually plump ("I was an elementary school Falstaff") winner of the 1989 Pulitzer Prize for Drama.*

There's nothing on earth to do here but look at the view and eat. You can imagine the result since I do not like to look at views.

—Famous wife **Zelda Fitzgerald**, *in a moment of jazz age angst. (Flappers were supposed to be flat, not fleshy.)*

If American men are obsessed with money, American women are obsessed with weight. The men talk of gain, the women talk of loss, and I do not know which talk is the more boring.

—Marya Mannes, *journalist/OSS intelligence analyst. Obviously, it didn't take her long to crack the nation's conversational code.*

I never worry about diets. The only carrots that interest me are the number you get in a diamond.

Too much of a good thing can be wonderful.

When women go wrong, men go right after them.

—Sex goddess **Mae West,** *honored in 1933 by the Central Association of Obstetricians and Gynecologists for "popularizing the natural plumpness of the female figure."*

I'm just a person trapped inside a woman's body.

—Comedian **Elayne Boosler**. *Rejected by the Joffrey Ballet school for being non-bulimic, she became a substantial "Showtime" star by default.*

Kiss my shapely big fat ass.

—Country crooner **K.T. Oslin**, *whose much-publicized menopause made her a trifle less petite, and far more impolite.*

Political
Animas
and
Public
Enemies

I want to be more than a rose in my husband's lapel.

I want two passports. I want a passport that says wife of the Prime Minister and a passport that says I'm free.

–**Margaret Trudeau**, a *sexy side-kick in the pants to her Studio 54 pals; a mondo thorn in the side for poor Pierre.*

Remember the Ladies, and be more generous and favorable to them than your ancestors. Do not put such unlimited power into the hands of the Husbands. Remember all Men would be tyrants if they could. If particular care and attention is not paid to the Ladies we are determined to foment a Rebellion, and will not hold ourselves bound by any Laws in which we have no voice, or Representation.

–Abigail Adams, *wife of the second president of the United States of America.*

Sometimes when I look at my children I say to myself, "Lillian, you should have stayed a virgin."

–Lillian Carter, *mother of the thirty-ninth president of the United States of America.*

Well, I've got you the presidency, what are you going to do with it?

–Florence Harding, *wife of the twenty-ninth president of the United States of America.*

33

Every politician should have been born an orphan and remain a bachelor.

–Lady Bird Johnson, *wife of the thirty-sixth president of the United States of America.*

If American politics are too dirty for women to take part in, there's something wrong with American politics.

–Writer **Edna Ferber**, *an ornery "old maid" who called them like she saw them.*

The position of First Lady has no rules, just precedent, so its evolution has been at a virtual standstill for years. If Martha Washington didn't do it, then no one is sure it should be done.

–Paula Poundstone, *social satirist with no political or marital ambitions whatsoever.*

I suppose I could have stayed home and baked cookies and had teas.

–Hillary Clinton, *wife of the forty-second president of the United States of America.*

35

One cannot be too extreme in dealing with social ills; besides, the extreme thing is generally the true thing.

There's never been a good government.

–Emma Goldman. *Often arrested for anarchy, "Red Emma" had plenty of solitary time to contemplate the numerous sins of the state.*

There is little place in the political scheme of things for an independent, creative personality, for a fighter. Anyone who takes that role must pay a price.

—**Shirley Chisholm**, *professor and practitioner of political science, and the first African-American woman to battle her way into Congress.*

I'm no lady; I'm a member of Congress, and I'll proceed on that basis.

—**Mary Norton**, *the first Democrat with breasts ever elected to Congress entirely on her own merits, rather than creeping in on the coattails of a deceased spouse.*

The test for whether or not you can hold a job should not be the arrangement of your chromosomes.

Our struggle today is not to have a female Einstein get appointed as an assistant professor. It is for a woman schlemiel to get as quickly promoted as a male schlemiel.

–**Bella Abzug**, *three-term U.S. Congresswoman from New York, known both for the unconventional contents of her cranium and her penchant for placing ladylike* chapeaux *on it.*

When people ask me why I am running as a woman, I always answer, "What choice do I have?"

I have a brain and a uterus, and I use both.

–Patricia Schroeder, *veteran Colorado congresswoman who coined the term "Tefloncoated presidency," also known as Mom.*

D r. Kissinger was surprised that I knew where Ghana was.

—Shirley Temple Black, *former Ambassador to Ghana. ("'The Good Ship Lollipop,'" all-grown-up Shirley once noted diplomatically, "is now in drydock.")*

W inning may not be everything, but losing has little to recommend it.

—Senator **Dianne Feinstein**, *the only powerhouse politico to dress for success in blouses with built-in bows.*

You can no more win a war than you can win an earthquake.

As a woman I can't go to war, and I refuse to send anyone else.

—Jeanette Rankin, *first woman to serve in Congress, and the sole member of either house to vote against U.S. entry into World War II.*

Man has been given his freedom to a greater extent than ever and that's quite wrong.

Everybody should rise up and say, "Thank you, Mr. President, for bombing Haiphong."

—Infamous Watergate wife **Martha Mitchell**, demonstrating the inherent nonviolent nature of womankind.

I'd like to see a women's army storm into the White House with Uzis and shotguns and eliminate at least half the population who work in politics. They're killing you slowly—what's the alternative? Kill them quickly, kill them now—before they kill everything else, okay?

–Lydia Lunch, *former vocalist for "Teenage Jesus and the Jerks," no longer sublimating her rage.*

Libidinous

Lingo

and

Tart

Retorts

All that you suspect about women's friendships is true. We talk about dick size.

–Cynthia Heimel, *well-informed author of* Sex Tips for Girls, *and evidently an excellent conversationalist as well.*

Women's virtue is man's greatest invention.

–Cornelia Otis Skinner, *author, actress, and the narrator of an informative NBC broadcast about debutantes in the sixties.*

The nicest women in our "society" are raving sex maniacs. But, being just awfully, awfully nice they don't, of course, descend to fucking—that's uncouth—rather they make love, commune by means of their bodies and establish sensual rapport.

—**Valerie Solanis**, *who furthered the feminist cause by founding SCUM (Society for Cutting Up Men) and attempting to assassinate Andy Warhol.*

There are two kinds of women: those who want power in the world, and those who want power in bed.

–Jacqueline Kennedy Onassis, *supremely successful serial monogamist.*

I wish I had as much in bed as I get in the newspapers.

–Linda Ronstadt, *prolific pop singer who posed the poignant musical question: "When Will I Be Loved?"*

A healthy sex life. Best thing in the world for a woman's voice.

–**Leontyne Price**, *world-renowned soprano.*

The prerequisite for making love is to like someone enormously.

–*Magazine editor* **Helen Gurley Brown**. *Yes, even those cleavage-baring* Cosmo *girls draw the line* somewhere!

I am a free lover!

–Victoria Woodhull, *the very unmarried candidate for the U.S. presidency in 1872, clarifying her official position on domestic relations.*

My reaction to porno films is as follows: After the first ten minutes, I want to go home and screw. After the first twenty minutes, I never want to screw again as long as I live.

–Erica Jong, *author of* Fear of Flying *(the seminal sexual liberation novel of the 1970s), once characterized by a fellow writer as "a mammoth pudenda."*

A mutual and satisfied sexual act is of great benefit to the average woman, the magnetism of it is health giving. When it is not desired on the part of the woman and she has no response, *it should not take place*. This is an act of prostitution and is degrading to the woman's finer sensibility, all the marriage certificates on earth to the contrary notwithstanding.

—Birth control pioneer **Margaret Sanger**, *in 1917. All in all, she was jailed nine times for her belief that offspring were optional.*

I've tried several varieties of sex. The conventional position makes me claustrophobic. And the others either give me a stiff neck or lockjaw.

–Tallulah Bankhead.
Even after considerable erotic experimentation, the agile actress remained (so she claimed) "as pure as the driven slush."

Until you've lost your reputation, you never realize what a burden it was or what freedom really is.

–Epic novelist **Margaret Mitchell**. *Evidently the antebellum South wasn't the only thing that was "Gone With the Wind."*

In my sex fantasy, nobody ever loves me for my mind.

—*Sizzling screenwriter* **Nora Ephron**, *actually (or so one interviewer assures us) "much prettier than she appears in most of her pictures."*

My own, or other people's?

—Peggy Guggenheim, *exceedingly amorous art patron, in response to the question "How many husbands have you had?"*

A different kind of dame gets a different kind of fame.

As far as I'm concerned, morality is just a word that describes the current fashion of conduct.

It seems to me that basically a woman who sells her emotions in bed, often pretending love and affection, is as great an actress as one who sells her beauty and emotions to the camera or the public. Personally, I trust most prostitutes further than the actresses I've known.

—**Sally Stanford**, *self-made madam and vice-mayor of Sausalito, California.*

I never made any money till I took off my pants.

—Exotic dancer **Sally Rand**, *famous for her well-placed fans.*

I ran the wrong kind of business, but I did it with integrity.

—Sidney Biddle Barrows, *the so-called "Mayflower Madam." Just as they say, breeding does indeed tell . . .*

The world wants to be cheated. So cheat.

Something is wrong here: sex has been with us since the human race began its existence, yet I would estimate that 90 percent of human beings still suffer from enormous inhibitions in this area.

–Xaviera Hollander, *a.k.a. "The Happy Hooker." Her bawdy Pill-era bestsellers provided millions of junior high virgins with useful information about mate-swapping, sex with other species, and amusing stunts to perform on public escalators.*

The real fountain of youth is to have a dirty mind.

My mother said it was simple to keep a man, you must be a maid in the living room, a cook in the kitchen and a whore in the bedroom. I said I'd hire the other two and take care of the bedroom bit.

Even if you have only two seconds drop everything and give him a blow job. That way he won't really want sex with anyone else.

—Jerry Hall, *former Texan model and vice versa, sharing her strategy for encouraging mate Mick Jagger to spend some quality time at home.*

Why do I show my cervix? I tell the audience that the reason I show my cervix is: 1) because it's fun—and I think fun is really important, and 2) because the cervix is so beautiful that I really want to share that with people.

–Annie Sprinkle, *former sex film star who now prefers to package her wholesome public exhibitions as performance art.*

Out
and
About

One thing I've noticed in particular about straight people—and I've known a lot of them so I think I can talk—is that when they find out you're lesbian, they inevitably ask, sooner or later, this famous question: "Why is it that so *many* lesbians dress like men?"

—**Kate Gawf**, *artist/writer who refrains from crass speculation on the relationship between sexual and sartorial orientation. She, for one, does not "sit around wondering whether the Pope has a boyfriend."*

I was eight years old and she [Eleanor Roosevelt] came to the Easter Egg Roll wearing jodhpurs and riding boots. I'm *sure* that had an influence on my life . . .

–Sally Gearhart, *graphic sapphic, speculating wildly on the origins of her sexual preference.*

I f you march around screaming "I'm a lesbian!" what good is it? I admire gay activists, but I'm an artist.

–k.d. lang, *Canadian-born chanteuse, who in 1993 apparently decided that coming out was better than acting out.*

Once you know what women are like, men get kind of boring. I'm not trying to put them down, I mean I like them sometimes as people, but sexually they're dull.

Lead me not into temptation; I can find the way myself.

—Rita Mae Brown. *Enough said. "Next time anybody calls me a lesbian writer," Ms. Brown once remarked, "I'm going to knock their teeth in."*

If you have one gay experience, does that mean you're gay? If you have one heterosexual experience, does that mean you're straight? Life doesn't work quite so cut and dried.

–Billie Jean King, *tennis champion who put a new spin on the phrase* love-all *when she copped to an extra-marital lesbian love affair. ("It's not contagious," Billie's highly-evolved husband assured the press. "I didn't catch it.")*

In the heterosexist imagination, everything that gay people do becomes sexualized. They think that's all we're doing, and unfortunately, it's not. I wish that being a lesbian were as juicy as I think Jesse Helms thinks it is.

—Holly Hughes, *obscenely unfunded performance artist who managed to steal a moment from her rigorous romantic schedule to sue the National Endowment for the Arts.*

Lesbians are "dykes," not "dikes." We are not dams, although some people consider us damned.

–**Margaret A. Robinson**, *sensitive speller, in a candid 1973 letter to Ms. about her alphabetical (and other) preferences.*

I'm everything you were afraid your little girl would grow up to be—and your little boy.

–**Bette Midler**. *The "Divine Miss M." launched her multi-faceted entertainment career in gay bath-houses.*

What is most beautiful in virile men is something feminine; what is most beautiful in feminine women is something masculine.

—**Susan Sontag**, *seductive intellectual once touted as the "Natalie Wood of the U.S. Avant Garde."*

The word [androgyny] is misbegotten—conveying something like "John Travolta and Farrah Fawcett-Majors scotch-taped together."

—**Mary Daly**, *the thinking woman's theologian.*

Coming from Nazi Germany and having survived Hitler and the concentration camps, I am very worried when I hear the word quarantine. Because the next thing they might decide is everyone 4'7" should be quarantined.

–Dr. Ruth Westheimer, *extra-small sex therapist, waxing wrathful over a proposal to segregate homosexuals and AIDS patients from the population at large.*

I think extreme hetero-sexuality is a perversion.

–Margaret Mead, *world-famous anthropologist who, having devoted her life to studying the ways of all flesh, was certainly in a position to know.*

As far as I'm concerned, being any gender is a drag.

–Rock singer **Patti Smith**, *who spent (perhaps not coincidentally) much of her youth reading Rimbaud and rapping with Robert Mapplethorpe.*

Vocal

Oracles

Y‍ou don't have to be dowdy to be a Christian.

–Tammy Faye Bakker, *ultra-lash evangelist. (Thou shalt not, however, skimp on eye-shadow.)*

I‍f I were going to convert to any religion I would probably choose Catholicism because it at least has female saints and the Virgin Mary.

–Margaret Atwood, *Canada's pre-eminent pagan novelist, poet, and "high priestess of angst."*

I learned that women were smart and capable, could live in community together without men, and in fact did not need men much.

—**Anna Quindlen**, *nun-educated essayist, on the feminist fringe benefits of attending parochial school.*

No good deed goes unpunished.

—**Clare Booth Luce**, *distinguished diplomat and a devout Catholic. (Before visiting the Vatican, Madam Ambassador had to swear to the Senate that she understood all about the separation of church and state.)*

The only sin is mediocrity.

–Martha Graham, *patron saint of modern dance.*

Every major horror of history was committed in the name of an altruistic motive. Has any act of selfishness ever equalled the carnage perpetrated by disciples of altruism?

–Rabid "radical capitalist" **Ayn Rand**, *who found the United States infinitely more congenial than post-revolutionary Russia.*

Most sermons sound to me like commercials—but I can't make out whether God is the Sponsor or the Product.

—**Mignon McLaughlin**, *self-confessed "neurotic." (Could channel-surfing be the cure?)*

The heresy of one age becomes the orthodoxy of the next.

—*Blind visionary* **Helen Keller**, *who saw some things more clearly than others.*

Conjugal

Confessions

and

Solitary

Digressions

Let's face it, when an attractive but ALOOF ("cool") man comes along, there are some of us who offer to shine his shoes with our underpants.

—Cartoonist **Lynda Barry**, *who completely understands that few women have anything in common with Sharon Stone.*

I require only three things of a man. He must be handsome, ruthless and stupid.

—**Dorothy Parker**, *whose minimal entrance requirements weren't precisely rigid. ("One more drink," the mistress of mal mots once confessed, "and I'd have been under the host.")*

A girl can wait for the right man to come along but in the meantime that still doesn't mean she can't have a wonderful time with all the wrong ones.

The trouble with some women is that they get all excited about nothing—and then marry him.

—**Cher**, *perennially popular entertainer. (After all, somebody's got to date the youth of America.)*

I never liked the men I loved, and I never loved the men I liked.

–**Fanny Brice**. *The leading lady of Ziegfeld's Follies had a few foibles (including a massive passion for a gangster) of her own.*

When he's late for dinner, I know he's either having an affair or is lying dead in the street. I always hope it's the street.

–**Jessica Tandy**, *married to fellow actor Hume Cronyn for nearly one-half century, on the subject of driving Miss Daisy completely bonkers.*

I have yet to hear a man ask for advice on how to combine marriage and a career.

I can't mate in captivity.

—**Gloria Steinem**, *the mother of all Ms's.*

To be killed or to be married is the universal female fate.

—Nineteenth-century author **Adele M. Fielde**. *In the deceptively decorous Victorian era, it was fatale not to be ultra-femme.*

When you see what some girls marry, you realize how they must hate to work for a living.

—Author **Helen Rowland**. *The woman who wrote* Reflections of a Bachelor Girl *had no aversion to applying herself.*

Any intelligent woman who reads the marriage contract, and then goes into it, deserves all the consequences.

—Isadora Duncan, *the flamboyant foremother of contemporary dance. Impulsive Isadora enjoyed many lovers, but her sole spouse committed suicide after two short years of matrimony.*

I have no wish for a second husband. I had enough of the first. I like to have my own way—to lie down mistress, and get up master.

—*Canadian pioneer* **Susanna Moodie**. *As a widow, she never got up on the wrong side of bed.*

Being alone and liking it is, for a woman, an act of treachery, an infidelity far more threatening than adultery.

—*Film critic* **Molly Haskell**, *who reviewed several scenes from a marriage (hers, not Bergman's) and concluded that romantic love was essentially an "infectious disease."*

One of the advantages of living alone is that you don't have to wake up in the arms of a loved one.

–Marion Smith, *who prefers to rest in peace.*

I don't need a man to rectify my existence. The most profound relationship we'll ever have is the one with ourselves.

–Shirley MacLaine, *frequently reincarnated actress who, over the centuries, has already had more than her fair share of fellows anyway.*

What a commentary on our civilization, when being alone is considered suspect; when one has to apologize for it, make excuses, hide the fact that one practices it—like a secret vice!

—Aviator/writer **Anne Morrow Lindbergh.** *Although happily wed to charming Charles, she envied nothing so much as the "austere peace" of monks.*

The world is my husband.

–Elsa Maxwell, *celebrated* bon vivant *who thought it perfectly possible to eat, drink and be unmarried.*

Sometimes I wonder if men and women really suit each other. Perhaps they should live next door and just visit now and then.

—Actress **Katharine Hepburn,** *who got along famously with married lover Spencer Tracy during a quarter-century of now-and-then visits.*

What ever happened to the kind of love leech that lived in his car and dropped by once a month to throw up and use you for your shower? Now all these pigs want is a *commitment.*

—Comedian **Judy Tenuta**, *the disgruntled, self-designated "Goddess of Love."*

Prolix
Professionals

What I wanted to be when I grew up was—in charge.

—Wilma Vaught, *Brigadier General of the U.S. Air Force.*

Give me my sword.

—Oveta Hobby, *first director of the Women's Army Corps, and a colonel nobody wanted to cross.*

The only jobs for which no man is qualified are human incubators and wet nurse. Likewise, the only job for which no woman is or can be qualified is sperm donor.

–Wilma Scott Heide,
R.N., enumerating the three textbook cases in which anatomy is indeed destiny.

I could have succeeded much easier in my career had I been a man.

—Financier **Henrietta Green**. Her anatomy notwithstanding, the "Witch of Wall Street" managed to invest her inheritance so shrewdly that she was acknowledged, at the turn of the century, as the wealthiest woman in the world.

I'm not surprised at what I've done.

—**Margaret Knight**, nineteenth-century inventor who patented more than two dozen types of heavy machinery.

Being a performer was always my destiny. When I was born, the doctors didn't have to pop me to get me going. It was like, "Thank you, thank you. I am here!" I was ready to party.

—*Comedic actress* **Whoopi Goldberg**, *full of* joie de vivre *from Day One.*

Broadway has been very good to me—but then I've been very good to Broadway.

—**Ethel Merman**. *During 1,147 performances of* Annie Get Your Gun, *the sharp-shooting showgirl managed to make her mark.*

My family wasn't the Brady Bunch. They were the Broody Bunch.

My father was a proctologist, my mother an abstract artist. That's how I see the world.

—Sandra Bernhard, *a magnificently maladjusted entertainer.*

I don't much enjoy looking at paintings in general. I know too much about them. I take them apart.

–Georgia O'Keeffe, *doyenne of the painted desert. Convent-educated O'Keeffe also didn't enjoy hearing about the sexual symbolism of her work, insisting that any putative crotch imagery was nothing but a crock.*

My favorite thing is to go where I've never been.

—Photographer **Diane Arbus**, *whose penchant for peculiar-looking posers led her down some rather unusual roads.*

Winning the prize wasn't half as exciting as doing the work itself.

—**Maria Goeppert Mayer**, *recipient of the 1963 Nobel Prize in physics.*

You come to doing what you do by not being able to do something.

–Grace Paley, *failed poet, acclaimed short story writer.*

I was thirty-seven, too old for a paper route, too young for social security, and too tired for an affair.

–Erma Bombeck, *on her transformation from housewife into humorist.*

I never thought I would fall on my face.

—*Califonia-cuisine queen* **Alice Waters.** *(And the soufflé also rises.)*

D ear, never forget one little point: It's my business. You just work here.

—**Elizabeth Arden.** *The queen bee of her own cosmetics empire, arrogant Arden refused to issue stock to her business manager/spouse.*

To love what you do and feel that it matters—how could anything be more fun?

–**Katharine Graham**, *extremely entertained publisher of the* Washington Post.

If I didn't start painting, I would have raised chickens.

–**Grandma Moses**, *a very pragmatic primitivist.*

Men,
Schmen

This book is dedicated to all those men who betrayed me at one time or another, in hopes they will fall off their motorcycles and break their necks.

—*Poet* **Diane Wakoski**, *graciously acknowledging the male muses who inspired her* Motorcycle Betrayal Poems.

If men can run the world, why can't they stop wearing neckties? How intelligent is it to start the day by tying a little noose around your neck?

—**Linda Ellerbee**, *broadcast journalist. Since her 1989 stint at the Betty Ford Clinic, the former darling of five networks has discontinued her own policy of tying one on daily. And so it goes.*

I don't have buried anger against men. Because my anger is right on the surface.

There is no female Mozart because there is no female Jack the Ripper.

–Camille Paglia. *As a child, the provocative Ph.D. hinted at her sexual persona-to-be by celebrating Halloween costumed as Napoleon, a Roman soldier, and the toreador from "Carmen."*

When a man gives his opinion he's a man. When a woman gives her opinion she's a bitch.

I am a woman meant for a man, but I never found a man who could compete.

–Bette Davis. *Off-screen, the star of* All About Eve *had a hard time scaring up a satisfactory Adam.*

If it's so natural to kill, why do men have to go into training to learn how?

–Joan Baez, *the world's most persistent peacenik.*

It's a man's world, and you men can have it.

–Katherine Anne Porter. *Though widely-travelled, the anarchistic novelist still wasn't a citizen of the world.*

The only time a woman really succeeds in changing a man is when he's a baby.

–Natalie Wood, *professional leading lady who failed to alter the behavior of beaux Elvis Presley, Warren Beatty, or Frank Sinatra.*

If boys are better, why should a male choose to love an inferior female? If a penis is so great, two penises should be even greater.

–Letty Cottin Pogrebin, *author of numerous feminist tomes, including* How To Make It In a Man's World *(first of all, it seems, it helps to be a man).*

Don't accept rides from strange men, and remember that all men are strange.

—*Writer* **Robin Morgan,** *who in a more separatist phase maintained that the* Sisterhood Is Powerful *enough to get there on its own unshaved legs.*

Whatever women do they must do twice as well as men to be thought half as good. Luckily, this is not difficult.

—**Charlotte Whitton,** *mathematically-gifted mayor of Ottawa.*

All men are rapists and that's all they are. They rape us with their eyes, their laws, and their codes.

–Marilyn French, *who plotted her counter-attack against the chauvinist conspiracy in* The Women's Room.

I wonder why men can get serious at all. They have this delicate long thing hanging outside their bodies, which goes up and down by its own will . . . If I were a man I would always be laughing at myself.

–Yoko Ono, *mature multi-media artist also amused by the gluteus maximus (her 1967 film* Bottoms, *for example, featured 365 bare posteriors).*

There aren't any hard women, only soft men.

–Raquel Welch, *notorious both for her annoyingly firm form and for her role as one-half of a transsexual character in the 1970 film* Myra Breckenridge.

I got it. I grabbed it by my right hand. And when I grabbed it, I gave it a yank. And when I yanked it, I twisted all at the same time.

–Curtescine Lloyd, *middle-aged Mississippian who refused to cooperate with a would-be rapist. Instead, Ms. Lloyd seized the assailant by the salient portion of his anatomy, squeezing insistently until he was incapable of committing the intended crime.*

Domestic
Dissidents

Whenever I date a guy, I think, is this the man I want my children to spend their weekends with?

—*Stand-up comic* **Rita Rudner**, *a person who likes to look at the big picture.*

Being a mother is a noble status, right? Right. So why does it change when you put "unwed" or "welfare" in front of it?

—*Civil rights lawyer* **Florynce Kennedy**, *once lionized by the press as "Radicalism's Rudest Mouth" and as a "loud-mouthed middle-aged colored lady" by herself.*

A printed card means nothing except that you are too lazy to write to the woman who has done more for you than anyone in the world. And candy! You take a box to Mother—and then eat most of it yourself. A pretty sentiment.

—**Anna Jarvis**, *founder of Mother's Day. In the end, she squandered Mom's entire estate on a campaign to prevent the Hallmarking of the holiday.*

I'm hostile to the act of childbirth — I've always found the concept of childbirth to be a morbid one at best — something *nostalgic* that a West Coast "return to nature" cult would espouse.

—Controversial composer **Diamanda Galás**, *simultaneously slammed by forty Italian newspapers for using her voice as "a tool of torture and destruction."*

I've been married to one Marxist and one Fascist, and neither one would take the garbage out.

—*Actress* **Lee Grant**. *Sorry to say, she never tied the knot with a member of the compost-conscious Green Party.*

In twenty years I've never had a day when I didn't have to think about someone else's needs. And this means the writing has to be fitted around it.

—**Alice Munro**, *child-bearing author.*

There's a time when you have to explain to your children why they're born, and it's a marvelous thing if you know the reason by then.

—Jazz musician **Hazel Scott**, *whose divorce from Congressman Adam Clayton Powell followed close on the heels of her performance in* The Night Affair.

I hate housework! You make the beds, you do the dishes—and six months later you have to start all over again.

—Joan Rivers, *chatty talk show host who gets more mileage out of her bust than her dustbuster.*

Housework isn't bad in itself—the trouble with it is that it's inhumanely lonely.

—**Pat Loud**, *ex-homemaker who enjoyed the constant company of in-house camera crews during the filming of* An American Family, *PBS' twelve-episode documentary chronicling the collapse of her marriage.*

I am a marvelous house-keeper. Every time I leave a man I keep his house.

—**Zsa Zsa Gabor**, *actress/property owner who, eight divorces notwithstanding, "has never hated a man enough to give him his diamonds back."*

I don't pretend to be an ordinary housewife.

—*The one and never-lonely* **Elizabeth Taylor***, presently married to an ordinary construction worker.*

Peeved
Eves

The militant, not the meek, shall inherit the earth.

Labor organizer **Mother Jones**, *one mean mama to mess with.*

A woman that's too soft and sweet is like tapioca pudding—fine for them as likes it.

—Osa Johnson, *jungle explorer who could cope with cobras, but not "the dangers of civilization."*

Of course I realized there was a measure of danger. Obviously I faced the possibility of not returning when first I considered going. Once faced and settled there really wasn't any good reason to refer to it.

–Amelia Earhart, *the first female aviator to soar successfully across the Atlantic, and the first to disappear without a trace while attempting to circumnavigate the globe.*

It's time to stop denying the "inner bitch" in ourselves. Stop apologizing for her. Set her free.

–Hysteria *magazine contributor* **Elizabeth Hilts**. *And the hell with the inner child!*

Once I decide to do something, I can't have people telling me I can't. If there's a roadblock, you jump over it, walk around it, crawl under it.

–**Kitty Kelley**, *extremely limber (and, according to some, extremely imaginative) celebrity biographer.*

Girlhood . . . is the intellectual phase of a woman's life, that time when, unencumbered by societal expectations or hormonal rages, one may pursue any curiosity from the mysteries of a yo-yo to the meaning of infinity. These two particular pursuits were where I left off in the fifth grade when I discovered a hair growing in the wrong place and all hell broke loose.

—Essayist and ex-nurse **Alice Kahn**. *Sans those secondary sex characteristics, she might have been the next Albert Einstein.*

When people keep telling you that you can't do a thing, you kind of like to try it.

–Margaret Chase Smith, *Maine politician who tried four terms in the U.S. House of Representatives and another four in the Senate.*

Life is either always a tight-rope or a feather bed. Give me the tight-rope.

–Edith Wharton, *stiff-spined Pulitzer Prize winner who deplored the vulgarity of post-Victorian America.*

I cannot and will not cut my conscience to fit this year's fashions.

I like people who refuse to speak until they are ready to speak.

—*Playwright* **Lillian Hellman,** *who declined an invitation to chat with the House Un-American Activities Committee in 1952.*

Slaying the dragon of delay is no sport for the short-winded.

—**Sandra Day O'Connor**, *aerobically-accomplished Supreme Court Justice.*

There is no female mind. The brain is not an organ of sex. Might as well speak of a female liver.

—**Charlotte Perkins Gilman**, *nineteenth-century activist who titled her autobiography* The Living [and not, one notes, The Liver] *of Charlotte Perkins Gilman.*

Nobody can make you feel inferior without your consent.

It's better to light a candle than to curse the darkness.

–Eleanor Roosevelt: *Her globe-trotting campaigns for good causes (and not her extra-marital mash on journalist Lorena Hickock) earned America's most-admired first lady the nickname of "Eleanor Everywhere."*

But oh, what a woman I should be if an able young man would consecrate his life to me as secretaries and technicians do to their men employers.

—**Mable Ulrich,** *early twentieth-century physician. (A wife would also have been nice.)*

If women can sleep their way to the top, how come they aren't there? . . . There must be an epidemic of insomnia out there.

—**Ellen Goodman,** *skeptical syndicated columnist.*

[W]omen] are early taught that to appear to yield, is the only way to govern.

I ask no favors for my sex . . . All I ask of our brethren is that they will take their feet from off our necks.

—Sarah Moore Grimké, *one of the first abolitionists to link the oppression of women with the oppression of slaves. (Ms. Grimke was not, however, the first individual to find patriarchal society a major pain in the neck.)*

I do not believe in sex distinction in literature, law, politics, or trade—or that modesty and virtue are more becoming to women than to men, but wish we had more of it everywhere.

–Belva Lockwood, *1884 presidential candidate who definitely did not have a Gary Hart problem. (Also, she definitely did not win the election.)*

I asked for bread, and got a stone in the shape of a pedestal.

Women have been called queens for a long time, but the kingdom given them isn't worth ruling.

–Louisa May Alcott, *a fierce feminist who resented her publisher's suggestion to write about* Little Women—*but not the resulting royalties.*

We, the people of the United States." Which "We, the people"? The women were not included.

—*Suffragist* **Lucy Stone**. *She took her semantics seriously, but not her husband's last name.*

To assess the damage is a dangerous act.

—*Playwright* **Cherrié Moraga,** *radical writer for a brave new world.*

Racy
Remarks

You can be up to your boo-
bies in white satin, with garde-
nias in your hair and no sugar
cane for miles, but you can still
be working on a plantation.

You've got to have some-
thing to eat and a little love in
your life before you can hold
still for any damn body's ser-
mon on how to behave.

–Billie Holiday, *who sang
like an angel, and saw more than
her share of hell.*

I do not weep at the world—
I am too busy sharpening my
oyster knife.

Sometimes, I feel discrimi-
nated against, but it does not
make me angry. It merely as-
tonishes me. How *can* any deny
themselves the pleasure of my
company? It's beyond me.

–Zora Neale Hurston,
*Barnard-educated belletrist of the
Harlem Renaissance.*

When I am alone I am not aware of my race or my sex, both in need of social contexts for definition.

–**Maxine Hong Kingston**, *not a woman warrior in private.*

I haven't seen anyone killed, and I have yet to kill anyone. I have exhibited *great restraint!*

–*Former "Days of Our Lives" staffer* **Wanda Coleman**, *who now prefers to write about black pride and prejudice instead of amnesia and adultery.*

There is nowhere you can go and only be with people who are like you. Give it up.

—*Cultural historian and founder of Sweet Honey in the Rock* **Bernice Johnson Reagon**. *(Ms. Reagon's own nonhomogeneous hangouts have included the curator's office at the National Museum of History, the stage of Carnegie Hall, and a jail cell following a student protest march.)*

My literary agenda begins by acknowledging that America has transformed *me*. It does not end until I show how I (and the hundreds of thousands like me) have transformed America.

—**Bharati Mukherjee**, *the first naturalized American citizen to win the National Book Critics Circle Award.*

Sometimes, it's like a hair across your cheek. You can't see it, you can't find it with your fingers, but you keep brushing at it because the feel of it is irritating.

–Marian Anderson, *on racism. Though the acclaimed singer debuted at the Metropolitan Opera, the Daughters of the American Revolution insisted she just wouldn't blend in with the color scheme at Constitution Hall.*

We do as much, we eat as much, we want as much.

—*Ex-slave and suffragist* **Sojourner Truth**. *Her name said it all.*

If they come for me in the morning, they will come for you at night.

—*African-American activist* **Angela Davis**, *formerly a fugitive on the FBI's "ten most wanted" list; now in great demand as a lecturer at institutions of higher education.*

Aged Sages

In our family we don't divorce our men—we bury them.

—Ruth Gordon, *whose* tour de force *as the septuagenarian seductress in* Harold and Maude *was a major turn-on for swinging audiences in the seventies.*

Age is something that doesn't matter, unless you are a cheese.

—Billie Burke, *aka Mrs. Flo Ziegfeld, cast as one of* The Young Philadelphians *at the ripe old age of seventy-four.*

The reason some men fear older women is they fear their own mortality.

I believe the second half of one's life is meant to be better than the first half. The first half is finding out how you do it. And the second half is enjoying it.

—Frances Lear, *founder/ editor of* Lear's, *the nation's only mass-circulation magazine for women too mature to have any genuine interest in advertisements for pimple cream.*

I'll be eighty this month. Age, if nothing else, entitles me to set the record straight before I dissolve. I've given my memoirs far more thought than any of my marriages. You can't divorce a book.

—*Silent screen superstar* **Gloria Swanson**. *In earlier days, she was the soul of discretion about her dalliance with Joseph P. Kennedy.*

Wisdom doesn't automatically come with old age. Nothing does—except wrinkles. It's true, some wines improve with age. But only if the grapes were good in the first place.

—Abigail Van Buren, *professional student of human nature; amateur viticulturist.*

I have bursts of being a lady, but it doesn't last long.

Now that I'm over sixty, I'm veering toward respectability.

—Well-seasoned sexpert **Shelley Winters**, *still making the rounds on the titillating talk-show circuit.*

Y ou cannot just waste time. Otherwise you'll die to regret it.

–**Harriet Doerr**, *who received her B.A. at the age of sixty-seven and published her first novel at seventy-four.*

I have everything I had twenty years ago, only it's all a little bit lower.

–Striptease artist **Gypsy Rose Lee***, pondering the ephemeral nature of perkiness.*

Phallus-Free

Philosophy

Reality is something you rise above.

–**Liza Minnelli**, *perpetually plagued by her problematic "z."*

Matter and death are mortal illusions.

–**Mary Baker Eddy**, *the deceased founder of the Church of Christian Science.*

Instant gratification takes too long.

—**Carrie Fisher**, *a major film star at the age of twenty-one.*

It is not true that life is one damn thing after another—it's one damn thing over and over.

—*Perturbed poet* **Edna St. Vincent Millay**. *(Burning the candle at both ends, it seems, doesn't really bring out the best in anyone.)*

The most popular labor-saving device is still money.

-Phyllis George, *sportscaster by trade, multi-millionaire by marriage.*

Only the little people pay taxes.

—*Hotel magnate* **Leona Helmsley**, *who eventually did time in the big house for tax evasion.*

Smoking kills. If you're killed, you've lost a very important part of your life.

—*Actress* **Brooke Shields**, *a Princeton graduate.*

Expiring for love is beautiful but stupid.

Lack of charisma can be fatal.

—**Jenny Holzer**, *internationally-acclaimed artist who actually earns a living inventing new cliches.*

N ever face facts; if you do you'll never get up in the morning.

—**Marlo Thomas**, *"That Girl" who played the role of TV's first independent career woman, only to wind up as the real-life wife of Phil Donahue.*

T here must be quite a few things a hot bath won't cure, but I don't know many of them.

—**Sylvia Plath**, *author of* The Bell Jar. *Her ultimate solution for psychic stress wasn't nearly as copasetic.*

If women ruled the world and we all got massages, there would be no war.

No day is so bad it can't be fixed with a nap.

—**Carrie Snow**, *stand-up comic who would really like to lie down for a while.*

Money has nothing to do with style at all, but naturally it helps every situation.

—*Fashion editor* **Diana Vreeland**. *Evidently big bucks keep the "Beautiful People" (a phrase coined by the voguish Ms. V.) from feeling blah.*

The art of being a woman can never consist of being a bad imitation of a man.

—Olga Knopf, *psychiatrist.*
Sometimes a cigar is just a cigar, but it's never a Virginia Slim.

Life itself is the proper binge.

—Chef **Julia Child**, *a top name in TV dinners.*

The trouble with the rat race is that even if you win, you're still a rat.

When we talk to God, we're praying. When God talks to us, we're schizophrenic.

Just remember, we're all in this alone.

–Lily Tomlin, *one of the few sure signs of intelligent life in the universe.*

Index

Also by Autumn Stephens

WILD WOMEN
Crusaders, Curmudgeons and Completely
Corsetless Ladies in the Otherwise
Virtuous Victorian Era

WILD WOMEN is a delightful collection of stories of over 150 women who refused to whittle themselves down to the 19th century notion of proper womanhood. Available by sending $12.95 plus $3 shipping and handling to the address above, or with a credit card, by calling 1-800-685-9595.

Autumn Stephens is the author of *WILD WOMEN: Crusaders, Curmudgeons, and Completely Corsetless Ladies in the Otherwise Virtuous Victorian Era.* A graduate of Stanford University, she lives in San Francisco. Her work has appeared in the *San Francisco Chronicle, SF Magazine,* and *various other publications.* She admires Fran Lebowitz and Madame de Staël, and is also indebted to Edna St. Vincent Millay for pointing out that "a person who publishes a book willfully appears before the populace with his pants down."